DATE DUE

D1275617

Turnip Soup

Lynne Born Myers
Christopher Myers

Illustrated by **Katie Keller**

Hyperion Books for Children
New York

For information address Hyperion Books for Children, 114 Fifth Avenue, New York, New York 10011.

First Edition
1 3 5 7 9 10 8 6 4 2

Library of Congress Cataloging-in-Publication Data
Myers, Christopher. Turnip soup / Christopher Myers, Lynne Born Myers; illustrated by Katie Keller.
p. cm.
Summary: George faces a troublesome Komodo dragon that has slithered into his family's root cellar and is eating all their vegetables.
ISBN 1-56282-445-7 (trade) — ISBN 1-56282-446-5 (lib. bdg.) [1. Komodo dragon — Fiction. 2. Lizards — Fiction.]
I. Myers, Lynne Born. II. Keller, Katie, ill. III. Title.
PZ7.M9825Tu 1994 [E] — dc20 93-11744 CIP AC

The illustrations for this book are pen-and-ink drawings colored with Dr. Ph. Martin's Water Colors.
This book is set in 14-point ITC Berkeley Old Style.

For Mildred Leona Wheatley, aka Meem
—L.B.M. and C.M.

For Uncle Karl
—K.K.

One afternoon in late summer, George stepped outside to pick up the evening newspaper, the *Beaufort Bugle*.

"Mom, watch out! There's a dragon on the loose!" George shouted as he ran into the kitchen.

"I'll keep my eyes peeled," George's mom promised. "But now I have to make potato soup. Please go down to the root cellar and get me six potatoes."

George stood at the top of the root-cellar stairs. Very large, muddy tracks led down into the murky shadows. Loud thumping and crunching sounds came from below.

"Mom! That dragon I mentioned is down in our root cellar!"

"Wasn't there a monster down there last week?"

"Not like this one."

"You'll just have to get rid of it," George's mom said. "And while you're at it, don't forget those potatoes for my potato soup."

"Well…," said George, "…if you say so."

George took one step down the stairs to the root cellar. A gnawed potato sailed past his head.

"Shoo!" George yelled. But nothing happened.

"Mom, I need a weapon. And I think the dragon has eaten all the potatoes. Can we have carrot soup instead?"

"If you'd rather have carrot soup, that's fine with me. But you'll have to get me a dozen carrots."

"What about the weapon?"

"Here," George's mom said, and she handed him the eggbeater.

"Thanks, Mom."

George took five slow steps into the root cellar.

"All right, dragon. I have an eggbeater. Don't make me use it," he called.

In a shaft of sunlight, George saw an *enormous* scaly tail scattering carrots and half-eaten potatoes across the cellar floor.

"Mom, the carrots are out. How about zucchini soup?"
"Fine, fine. Just get me some vegetables!"
"I need a shield. The dragon's much bigger than I thought."
"Take this." George's mom handed him the lid to the roasting pan.

"He may be a fire breather," George said.

"Take my oven mitt," his mom said, "so you can hold the shield if it gets too hot."

"Thanks, Mom."

George crept ten steps down the cellar stairs. The dragon's head was buried in a bushel of zucchini.

"Ugh!" George exclaimed at the sight of the dragon's huge, knobby body.

The dragon froze. Then, ever so slowly, it swung its head around, bushel and all, and took one heavy step toward George.

"Sorry, Mom, the dragon got the zucchini."

"Oh, for Pete's sake, George. Aren't you overdoing this?"

"I can't help it, Mom. This is one hungry dragon."

"OK, OK. Get me some mushrooms and I'll make mushroom soup."

"I'll need a helmet," George said.

"Take my mixing bowl," she answered.

George boldly descended to the very bottom step. The dragon was reaching for the mushrooms on the top shelf. The shelf teetered, rocked, then fell with a tremendous crash.

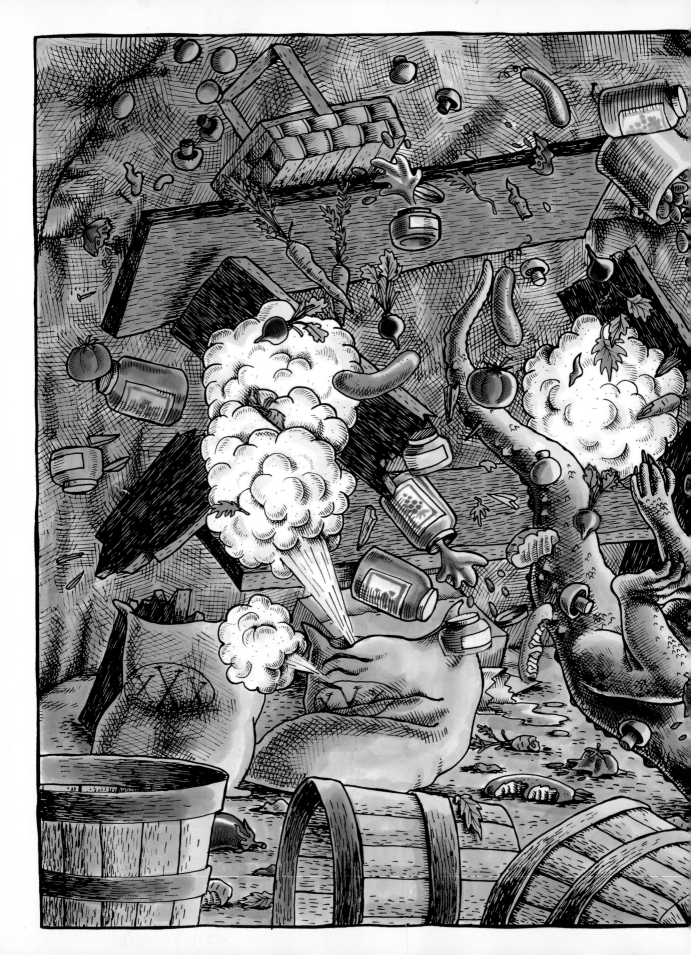

Cucumbers bounced.
Tomatoes squashed.
Beets rolled.
Jam splattered.
Flour flew everywhere!

"Mom, the only food left in the cellar is a bag of turnips. I guess we'll have to have turnip soup."

"But you don't even like turnip soup," she said. "I'm putting a stop to this nonsense! I'll go with you this time."

"You'll need armor," George said.

"I'm dragonproof," she replied.

"I'm not sure I am," said George.

"Here, put these cookie sheets under your shirt and we'll go get some vegetables."

George's mom gaped at the cellar. What a mess! "George, what have you been…" Then she saw the Komodo dragon. The big beast lay against a burlap bag. It clutched three turnips in one scaly foot. The dragon gnashed its jagged teeth.

As she grabbed George's hand and they retreated up the cellar steps, she whispered, "Let's just call out for pizza!"